THE 2026 OFF BROAD STREET SHORT PLAY FESTIVAL

Edited by
Jonathan Cook

THE 2026 OFF BROAD STREET SHORT PLAY FESTIVAL

Cover & Book Design: Jonathan Cook
First Edition: April 2026
ISBN: 978-1-964045-15-3

The 3rd Annual Off Broad Street Short Play Festival took place in April 2026 at Le Chat Noir Theatre in Augusta, GA.

The casts were as follows:

DRESSING BOBBY STRONG
Written by Stephen Spotswood
Directed by Tommy Cooper
Cast
BOBBY – Wesslen Romano
CONSTANCE – Korilyn Hendricks

HEAVEN HELP ME
Written by Jaclyn Stiller
Directed by Tracy Cook
Cast
NUN – Lillie DeLecuona
DEVIL – Anna Romano

KAYLEE AND ADELYN
Written by Elizabeth Shannon
Directed by TJ McSherry
Cast
KAYLEE – Carlee McClary
ADELYN – Madison Junod

MADAM TIFFANI, THE MINOR ARCANE
Written by Michael Lin
Directed by Karla Daly
Cast
TIFFANI – Maisie Bailey
DUCKY – Jackson Sample
ANDY – Tricia Perea

MISSED DISCONNECTIONS
Written by Samara Siskind
Directed by TJ Reissner
<u>*Cast*</u>
BEN – Travis Campfield
SLOAN – Ashanti Friels-Paz
MARGOT – Madeline Eaton

SNACKS, DRUGS, AND THE SEXUAL APPETITE OF THE GAYS
Written by Steven G. Martin
Directed by Lillie DeLecuona
<u>*Cast*</u>
AIDEN – Wesley Pierson
JAKE – Rico Weiland
MERLE – Blake McGee
CATHLEEN – Carlee McClary
GWEN – Andy Middleton

STEPHEN HAWKING'S TRAIN
Written by Mike Byham
Directed by Paris S. Pringle
<u>*Cast*</u>
PERSON 1 – Michell Davis
PERSON 2 – Troy Lewis
PERSON 3 – Andy Middleton

THE DIARY OF MARIA
Written by Dave Huber
Directed by Arelis Rivera
<u>*Cast*</u>
MARIA – Ava Robinson
MR. HARRIS – Blake McGee

WHEN I SORROW MOST
Written by Amy Patton
Directed by TJ Reissner
<u>*Cast*</u>
ANA – Karla Daly
MARK – Tracy Cook

Table of Contents

DRESSING BOBBY STRONG

by Stephen Spotswood

It's Constance's first time dressing the deceased in her new job as funeral director's apprentice and the body on her table is Bobby, a long-lost friend from high school. As she helps Bobby into his last suit of clothes, she remembers why he was one of the few bright spots during a traumatic time in her life. A sweet, sad story about love and mortality.

CHARACTERS

BOBBY
    male, mid-20s; dead

CONSTANCE
    female, mid-20s; an atheist, a former high school wallflower, a funeral director in training.

SETTING

The back room of a funeral home; the memory and imagination of a woman who used to be a seventeen-year-old girl who never took the chances she desperately wanted to.

DRESSING BOBBY STRONG by Stephen Spotswood

***

Lights up on a cold, sterile room.

The body of Bobby lies on a table. Next to the table is a single chair. Atop the chair is a carefully folded arrangement of clothes: dress shirt, pants, socks, shoes, jacket, cuff links. There are three ties. There is also a bottle of baby powder.

Bobby is wearing only a pair of underwear. His body is covered from feet to neck in a white, linen sheet.

Constance enters and approaches the table.

CONSTANCE. Hi Bobby.

(Constance pulls the sheet off Bobby.)

So, I thought you should know. You're my first. Mister Halloway should have had me doing this weeks ago. I don't think he trusts assistants.

That's not true. I don't think he trusts female assistants. He thinks I'm going to faint the first time I touch a body.

(She touches him.)

Look. No fainting.

Do you mind if I talk to you?

In school they teach us that talking to the deceased is respectful. And calming. For me, not for you. Obviously.

So do you mind?

(Bobby shakes his head.)

Good.

(She picks up the bottle of powder and sprinkles it on Bobby then begins rubbing it evenly across his body.)

This is so the clothes go on easy. They used to use talcum, but the smell was too strong. People would be all like, "Why does grandma smell like a barbershop?" Unscented baby powder. It smells nice. Like childhood.

Roll over for me. I need to get your back.

(Bobby rolls onto his side. Constance applies powder to the back of his body.)

Thank you.

You probably don't remember me. Connie Burrows? But you never called me Connie. It was always Constance. Always very formal.

When Mister Halloway said the client's name was Robert Strong, I didn't even think. I was so used to calling you Bobby. Did you turn into a Robert in college? I wouldn't be surprised. You were always so serious.

You can roll back.

(He returns to his back.)

But can I still call you Bobby?

(He nods.)

Thanks.

(She begins unfolding his clothes.)

Mister Halloway cuts the clothes up the back. I think it's a shame. Spend so much time picking out a nice suit just to have some old man take shears to it. I'm not going to cut it. But you've got to help me, okay?

(He nods.)

Okay. Up you go.

(He sits up. He allows her to lift his legs, guide his limbs – a willing marionette. As she speaks, she slips his pants on.)

My first day at school, I saw you and you were wearing a tie. A vest and a tie. It was so...mature. There's someone else who's desperate to get out of here, I thought. To have all the messy business of growing up over and done.

BOBBY. Can I help you?

CONSTANCE. What?

BOBBY. You look lost.

CONSTANCE. It's my first day. I'm looking for Room 310. Biology with Ms. Reeder.

BOBBY. I took her class last year. It's cool.

CONSTANCE. Yeah?

BOBBY. Yeah. You get to dissect a fetal pig.

CONSTANCE. Ew.

BOBBY. You can opt out.

CONSTANCE. Good. I can't stand dead animals.

BOBBY. Don't blame you. But you're on the wrong side of the building. You need to go to the end of the hall, make a left, go to the end of that hall where the stairs are, head up two flights, and it's right in front of you.

CONSTANCE. End of the hall. Left. End of that hall. Up the stairs. Thanks.

BOBBY. I'm Bobby, by the way. Bobby Strong.

CONSTANCE. Constance Burrows. Um...

BOBBY. What?

CONSTANCE. You've got a draft.

BOBBY. A what?

CONSTANCE. Your fly's down.

BOBBY. Shit.

   (He zips up.)
   Thanks!

CONSTANCE. Just returning the favor.
   Shoes and socks now?

DRESSING BOBBY STRONG by Stephen Spotswood

(She retrieves his shoes and socks from the chair and begins putting them on him.)

When Dad asked if I made any friends my first day, I was able to say yes. Though I guess that was a lie. We were never really friends, were we? Dad said it was good I make friends. He said we were going to be living there for a long while and I should find people my own age to spend time with. I didn't need to stay at home all the time with him. He promised me the cancer center was the best in the country and they were going to make him all better.

(She retrieves his undershirt from the chair and begins helping him into it. Then she moves on to his dress shirt – stark white with French cuffs.)

See? He lied to me, too. That's what people do when they love each other. They lie. I think that's why I felt the way I did about you. You lied to me.

BOBBY. Love the new glasses.

Great job on the presentation. If I need tutoring, I guess I know who to ask.

Don't listen to her. Janine's just jealous she can't get her hair to do that.

CONSTANCE. You were good at it, too. Maybe you talked to me two dozen times that year. Less. Every time for just the briefest of moments, it made me feel like ... somebody who wasn't me.

French cuffs. I love French cuffs.

(She retrieves the cufflinks and begins expertly attaching them.)

Dad wore them every Sunday to church. I put them on for him after his hands started shaking too much. I stopped going with him, though. He told me I shouldn't be angry with God. That he wasn't to blame.

(She looks at the three ties.)

What do you think? The red? No. Blue. It brings out your eyes.

(She ties his tie for him.)

I wish I was angry with God.

I went back to school because I thought this was what I wanted to do. That this work would help give me purpose. Meaning.

Do you see any meaning here?

(No answer from Bobby.)

No answer.

Mister Halloway says people who come here – they want to believe they'll see their loved ones again, talk to them, walk with them. Get another chance to do and say all the things they didn't. They don't want anyone telling them they won't. They don't want anyone telling them that this is the end. This is all they get. Everything else is a fantasy.

(She retrieves his vest and slips it on him.)

You look just like you did at the spring formal. Dad was really bad that week, but he said I needed to go. "You'll cherish those memories someday, Connie."

Do you remember me there? Probably not. I sat in a corner table by myself and watched everyone.

Especially you.

(She retrieves his jacket and helps him into it. There's the faint sound of music, fun and fast.)

Moving from table to table, talking, laughing. But you weren't dancing. You'd look out on the dance floor and smile. But you didn't go and join. Why didn't you go out there?

I wanted to. I rehearsed it in my head. What I'd say?

BOBBY. Hey, Constance. You having fun?

CONSTANCE. Yeah. You?

BOBBY. So far.

CONSTANCE. Do you want to dance?

BOBBY. No thanks. Two left feet. I'd just embarrass myself.

CONSTANCE. Me, too. I mean, I don't dance either.

BOBBY. Four left feet total. Doesn't sound like a good combination.

CONSTANCE. I don't know. Maybe it wouldn't be so bad. We can be embarrassed together.

BOBBY. Okay. But if I step on your toes, you asked for it.

CONSTANCE. I know.

(The music changes to something slow.)

BOBBY. Uh-oh. Slow dance. You still want to?

CONSTANCE. Yes.

(They dance. It is beautiful and flawless like only a seventeen-year-old girl's imagination can make it.)

You're all sweat and sweet cologne. You make me forget about home and the smell of the cancer and the chemo.

BOBBY. You're pretty good.

CONSTANCE. You're not so bad yourself. Do you mind if I kiss you?

BOBBY. I'd like that.

(They're about to kiss when the music stops. He returns to the table and sits down.)

CONSTANCE. Dad died that April. I went to live with my sister and her husband. And you went off to become Robert.

(She begins buttoning and straightening and tucking.)

I lied, by the way. You aren't my first. My father was. I'd been helping him get dressed for so long, I wouldn't let anyone else do it. Right before he died, he said, "We'll see each other again, Connie."

That's how I knew he still loved me.

(She helps him lie back down.)

High school. Dances. Kisses. One chance, and then it's gone.

Do you mind if I kiss you?

(He remains still. She kisses him. She straightens his tie, brushes the hair out of his eyes.)

You look beautiful.

(She turns around and walks away.)

END OF PLAY

HEAVEN HELP ME

by Jaclyn Stiller

Two unlikely strangers spark a friendship as they wait for their bus on Halloween night, finding that their clothes don't tell their whole story.

CHARACTERS

NUN
   A quiet and calm presence. 30s-40s, female presenting.

DEVIL
   The life of the party. 20s-30s, any gender.

SETTING

A bus stop bench in the early evening of Halloween night.

HEAVEN HELP ME by Jaclyn Stiller

***

At rise, Nun approaches the bus stop and sits on the bench, dressed in a traditional habit. She hums/sings "It's Raining Men" by The Weather Girls in a good-mood sort of way. She checks her watch, peers around to anticipate the bus, and pulls out her rosary beads while she waits. A few moments pass.

Devil runs up to the bus stop, hoping they didn't miss it. They are wearing a Spirit Halloween-quality Devil's costume that is sufficiently slutty and complete with plastic red devil horns. They look around for the bus, panting. Nun shyly stops her humming as soon as she is no longer alone.

DEVIL. Did I miss the Gray Line?

NUN. Bus is late.

DEVIL. Oh, thank God.

    (Sits down on the bench.)

NUN. Are you going to a Halloween party?

DEVIL. Yeah. You?

NUN. Going home.

DEVIL. Already? It's barely dark.

NUN. I've been out all day.

DEVIL. Right on. Well, I like your costume.

NUN. *(pauses)* Thank you. I've gotten a lot of use out of it. I like your costume.

DEVIL. Oh, thanks. My friend who I'm meeting at the party is dressed as an angel, but now I think I should have made him dress up as a nun.

NUN. You didn't want to dress as the angel?

DEVIL. No, devil's more fun.

NUN. I suppose that is the general consensus.

15

DEVIL. Plus it's way easier to be a sexy devil. I wouldn't even know how to make a nun outfit sexy.

(Realizes how that sounded.)

Not that your costume isn't sexy! It's very sexy. In a subtle, demure kind of way.

NUN. That's…kind of you to say.

DEVIL. Did you do a group costume with anyone?

NUN. My sisters and I.

DEVIL. Aw that's so cute. I think the last time I did matching costumes with my sister, I was 7 and we were Sarah Palin and Hilary Clinton.

NUN. Oh!

DEVIL. My parents were really involved in caucusing for Obama.

NUN. Are you close with your sister?

DEVIL. Um, yeah close enough. You know how sisters are.

NUN. I do. Do you live around here?

DEVIL. Yeah, I'm over on Oxford. You?

NUN. St. Benedict's on 32nd.

DEVIL. Oh, near that church?

NUN. Very near.

(Pause.)

Do you always dress as the devil for Halloween?

DEVIL. No, last year I went as a piñata.

NUN. How does one dress as a piñata?

DEVIL. You mostly just wear a lot of bright colors and then throw candy at people when they whack you with a stick.

NUN. I see.

DEVIL. What were you last year?

NUN. I'm always a nun.

DEVIL. Every year?

NUN. Every day.

DEVIL. Oh. Oh. Oh, nooooooo. I'm sorry, I just assumed –

NUN. It's perfectly fine. I had actually forgotten what day it was until you sat down.

DEVIL. How long have you been a nun?

NUN. 7 years.

DEVIL. Wow, that's a long time to be…I mean I just don't know if I could…don't you miss sex?

NUN. *(laughs)* Um, well, is it hard to be celibate? It can be. I think at different moments in my life, it's been more difficult than other times. I just choose to express love in different ways.

DEVIL. Oh my God, I'm sorry, was that a rude question? Am I not supposed to ask that?

NUN. *(smiling)* It's fine.

DEVIL. I don't always think before I speak. You can ask me something personal if you want. Make it even.

NUN. Oh … alright. Let's see, something personal. What is it that you believe in?

DEVIL. That is a good question, I probably should have an answer. *(clearly thinking of it on the spot)* Be nice to other people. Um, don't litter. And just, like, have fun. I think people take things way too seriously. Honestly, I think everyone should just have as much fun as we can in this short life, and like, do no harm. Doesn't have to be more complicated than that. *(turns to Nun)* I mean, do we really go to heaven or hell after we die?

NUN. I don't know. I wish I knew. I've never met anyone who's died and come back to life to tell me. But I really hope there's a place called Heaven. A place that is complete and good that we can come home to. What do you think?

DEVIL. Heaven sounds nice. But if there's a hell, I hope it's empty.

NUN. Me too.

(Pause.)

Well, as long as we're just waiting here. Do you have any other questions for me you'd like to know? You ask some good ones.

DEVIL. *(thinks for a moment)* Have you ever had a crush on someone?

NUN. Yes, I have. In fact, I've known some nuns who have had crushes while they've been nuns.

DEVIL. Stop it, really?

NUN. We are human beings, after all. We have sexuality. We have feelings.

DEVIL. Do you have a celebrity crush?

NUN. I think there are many talented actors who are a joy to watch on –

DEVIL. Come on, there's got to be someone that you –

NUN. *(interrupting)* Bradley Cooper.

DEVIL. Nice choice.

NUN. Nice eyes. Who is your celebrity crush?

DEVIL. Orlando Bloom, or Kiera Knightley. It's a tossup.

NUN. I can see that.

DEVIL. Have you ever been in love?

NUN. Yes.

(Devil waits for Nun to elaborate. She doesn't.)

DEVIL. I think it's your turn to ask a question.

NUN. Who is your favorite person in your life?

DEVIL. *(smiles)* My grandpa. I haven't seen him in a while. But he's so cool, rides a motorcycle and has a gold tooth and refuses to wear sunscreen. He reminds me a little bit of Harrison Ford, just kind of this badass. Oops! *(covers mouth)* Sorry for swearing.

NUN. I don't give a fuck.

DEVIL. So you wear that every day, huh? Do you just have the one?

NUN. No, of course not. I have two!

DEVIL. Wow. I guess it makes getting dressed in the morning pretty easy.

NUN. I took a vow of poverty. It means I chose a simpler life.

DEVIL. Does the rest of the world seem really selfish to you then?

NUN. No, that's not it at all. This is just…my way of doing no harm.

(Nun sneezes.)

DEVIL. Bless you.

NUN. Thank you.

(Beat.)

Am I the first nun you've ever met?

DEVIL. I think so. I've met some priests, back when I went to Catholic school. Never any nuns.

NUN. Where'd you go to Catholic school?

DEVIL. St. Joseph's.

(Nun nods in recognition)

I went there through 5th grade, but then my parents pulled me out because of all the abuse cases in the news. We stopped going to church altogether after that. That was the last year I saw my grandpa. He didn't want to see us after that.

NUN. Because your family left the Church?

DEVIL. *(nods)* He thought my parents were ruining me.

Hey, maybe he was right. I can't help but wonder what he would think of me now. I don't think I'm what he hoped I would be.

NUN. I'm very sorry to hear that.

DEVIL. It's a tough thing when your favorite person in the world doesn't really like you. And all because of some religion that claims it's about love but then makes families hate each other. It's just bullshit.

NUN. You're right, that isn't loving. I can see why you wouldn't be a fan of religion.

DEVIL. At least not yours. Sorry. But really, that institution has done some really awful shit. Like, how do you…

NUN. You can ask me.

DEVIL. How can you still belong to something like that? Don't you see how messed up it is?

NUN. *(thoughtful pause)* Have you ever loved someone who has disappointed you? And despite hating their actions, you can't help but still have love for the person anyway?

It's hard to explain. I'm deeply angry – and sad – for things the Church has done. The ways it has harmed people. Silenced people. Kept people out. It is run by humans, which means it is deeply imperfect. But I still have hope that it can do good things. You're right. We have a lot of work to do to live out the faith we say we believe. Maybe my vocation is to try to make things better from within its walls, and, I don't know, be a different representation of my faith to the world.

It's not a perfect answer, I know.

DEVIL. You're doing your best, I suppose. I can't fault you for that.

NUN. Do you think it's possible to be friends with someone you disagree with?

DEVIL. I do, most of the time. Depends on what you

disagree on.

NUN. Like?

DEVIL. I'm happy to disagree with someone on a million things; how the universe works, what happens after we die, if we were all insects in another life. But I'm not going to have a conversation with someone if their beliefs question my humanity. Like if your core beliefs tell you that I'm less than human, I won't talk to you. Because if I did, I'd be betraying myself. Like hell am I doing that.

NUN. That's a very good line to draw. I wholeheartedly agree with that.

DEVIL. Has anyone ever been rude to you because of your religion?

NUN. Oh, yes. The other day, there was a person who approached me. He had a bad experience in the Church, and I think he wanted to take that out on someone. The fact is, by wearing this habit, I do represent the Church. But it wasn't a big deal, and I pray for him.

DEVIL. What did he say to you?

NUN. He spat on me. Said some terrible words, stood quite close to me. It wasn't the first time someone was rude, but it was the first time in my 7 years as a nun that I've been truly afraid.

DEVIL. I'm sorry that happened to you.

NUN. But that's life, isn't it? I suppose if I'm treated badly, it gives me a sense of empathy with others who are treated badly.

DEVIL. Do you ever regret becoming a nun?

NUN. No, I don't regret it. But I have questioned it. When I entered the monastery, I was a different person than I am now. And life has a lot of ups and downs that shape you. But this is the best way I know how to live my life.

DEVIL. I think I'm living the best way I know how to live mine too.

(Points to Nun as if to say "your turn".)

NUN. So, your friend the angel. Is he a friend, or a…?

DEVIL. *(laughs nervously)* Uh, right now he's a friend. But we'll see how the night goes. I was sort of hoping the devil costume would give me a little confidence.

NUN. I'm sure he'll love it.

(Points in a similar "your turn" gesture.)

DEVIL. Which is the better movie: Sound of Music, or Sister Act?

NUN. What! Oh, that's an impossible choice! *(thinks hard, this is the toughest question she's received so far)* Sister Act 2: Back in the Habit.

DEVIL. Excellent choice.

(Headlights of a bus approach from the distance.)
Finally.

(Gathers their things.)
Are you getting on?

NUN. No, mine is the next one. Enjoy your party.

DEVIL. *(pauses)* Would you like to come?

NUN. Me? No, I can't.

DEVIL. Nuns don't drink?

NUN. Oh, we do. But it's movie night at the monastery tonight, and we're watching The Exorcist.

DEVIL. Next time then. I hope you get home safe.

(Devil stands to go, then turns back to Nun.)
How do you know it's all real? God, and all that.

NUN. I don't. I have no hard proof, nothing to tell me definitively. But for me, I just know there's something more. And I hope it's real.

(The bus brakes squeal. Doors open.)
You should tell that angel boy how you feel.
DEVIL. Okay, I will. Pray for me.

END OF PLAY

KAYLEE AND ADELYN

by Elizabeth Shannon

Two twins go through life together before gun violence tears them apart.

CW: school shooting, gun violence

CHARACTERS

KAYLEE MAE SHAW
  identical twin to Adelyn. First place.

ADELYN FRANCES SHAW
  identical twin to Kaylee. Second place.

NOTE: The actors playing KAYLEE and ADELYN need not be identical.

.

SETTING

The shared connection of Kaylee and Adelyn. An otherworldly space. A high school. America. Present.

***

Kaylee and Adelyn stand on a nearly blank stage. They are downstage center, next to each other. Behind them, one on stage right and one on stage left, are two high school desk chairs.

KAYLEE. Kaylee.

ADELYN. And Adelyn.

KAYLEE. Inseparable.

ADELYN. Basically the same person.

KAYLEE/ADELYN. *(together)* Except not really.

KAYLEE. Kaylee.

ADELYN. And Adelyn.

KAYLEE. Kaylee Mae.

ADELYN. And Adelyn Frances.

KAYLEE/ADELYN. *(together)* Shaw.

KAYLEE. Kaylee.

ADELYN. And Adelyn.

KAYLEE/ADELYN. *(together)* Were born on October 22nd, 2004, at 4:53 AM.

KAYLEE. Well, Kaylee was.

ADELYN. Adelyn was born six minutes later.

KAYLEE/ADELYN. *(together)* 4:59 AM.

KAYLEE. Kaylee was older.

ADELYN. But Adelyn was just a hairrrrrr taller.

KAYLEE. Kaylee got everything.

ADELYN. At least Adelyn secretly thought so.

KAYLEE. Kaylee Mae had the prettier middle name.

ADELYN. Adelyn Frances was just an afterthought.

KAYLEE. The name picked out of a baby book.

ADELYN. When their parents found out they were having twins.

KAYLEE. But nobody needed to know that.

ADELYN. Except everyone could almost tell.

KAYLEE. How one was always.

ADELYN. Second place.

KAYLEE/ADELYN. *(together)*
Except they were
Identical twins
Very incredibly identical
Absolutely no way to tell them apart.

KAYLEE. To this day, no one can.

ADELYN. They think their best friend, Giana, just guesses.

KAYLEE/ADELYN. *(together)* They respond to both.

KAYLEE. Even their parents.

ADELYN. "Are you –

KAYLEE. Kaylee…

ADELYN. Or Adelyn?"

KAYLEE. Kaylee.

ADELYN. And Adelyn.

KAYLEE/ADELYN. *(together)* Have all the same hobbies.

KAYLEE. Figure skating.

ADELYN. Then dance.

KAYLEE. Then somehow…

ADELYN. Soccer.

KAYLEE. Kaylee is goalie.

(Kaylee mimes being a goalie.)

ADELYN. Adelyn is striker.

(Adelyn mimes being a striker.)

KAYLEE/ADELYN. *(together)* The only way to tell them apart.

KAYLEE. Boys won't date them.

ADELYN. They're scared.

KAYLEE. The girls would trick them.

ADELYN. Which is fair –

KAYLEE/ADELYN. *(together)* They probably would.
> *(Kaylee and Adelyn laugh in perfect unison. Maybe they high-five.)*

KAYLEE. Kaylee.

ADELYN. And Adelyn.

KAYLEE. Your –

ADELYN. Perfect –

KAYLEE/ADELYN. *(together)* Sideshow-esque twins.

KAYLEE. We aren't conjoined.

ADELYN. Maybe if we were Kaylee'd be a better goalie
> *(Kaylee playfully slaps Adelyn's arm.)*

KAYLEE/ADELYN. *(together)* But people basically look at us like we're glued together.

KAYLEE. Kaylee.

ADELYN. And Adelyn.

KAYLEE. "Freaks".

ADELYN. "Half a brain in each of them".

KAYLEE. "Impossible to tell apart".

ADELYN. "Does Adelyn ever even talk?"
> *(Moment.)*

KAYLEE. It's probably hard.

ADELYN. When you're the "and".

KAYLEE. Kaylee.

ADELYN. And – Adelyn.

KAYLEE. Kaylee.

ADELYN. And – Adelyn.

KAYLEE. Always the first.

ADELYN. Always the afterthought.

KAYLEE. And what would it have been like –

ADELYN. If our parents had said –

KAYLEE/ADELYN. *(together)* Adelyn and Kaylee.

(The girls look at each other. They shiver, pretend to vomit, etc. Then they laugh.)

Weird.

(Kaylee and Adelyn sit in their respective high school desk chairs.)

KAYLEE. Kaylee.

ADELYN. And Adelyn.

KAYLEE. Don't have the same schedule.

ADELYN. It was mostly for their teacher's sake.

KAYLEE/ADELYN. *(together)* No one could ever learn who was who. So, for a brief moment, they are –

KAYLEE. Kaylee (and Adelyn).

KAYLEE/ADELYN. *(together)* And –

ADELYN. (Kaylee and) Adelyn.

KAYLEE/ADELYN. *(together)* Instead of –

KAYLEE. Kaylee.

ADELYN. And Adelyn.

KAYLEE. And on October 5th, 2022.

ADELYN. Just 17 days short of their 18th birthdays.

KAYLEE. Kaylee was sitting in Calculus.

ADELYN. And Adelyn was sitting in AP Lang.

KAYLEE/ADELYN. *(together)* When…

(Simultaneous blackout and BANG!)

(Moment. Lights rise on Adelyn, cowered behind her desk chair. The faint sounds of ambulances, and maybe

screaming, in the distance. Kaylee is gone. Adelyn looks around and slowly, slooooowly, stands. She's waiting. She's waiting for Kaylee to start. There is a very long silence.)

ADELYN. Kaylee?

(There is a very long silence again. Adelyn drops to her knees.)

And Adelyn.

Adelyn.

Just.

Adelyn.

…

(Adelyn looks to the spot Kaylee used to stand in. Blueout. Adelyn stands and returns to where she stood in the opening.)

Some people

Not at school, but other places

They don't know better

They ask

"Are you Kaylee or Adelyn?"

Or just

"Are you Kaylee?"

She always got out more.

But no.

I am Adelyn.

And then they ask, "Oh, what's Kaylee up to? Why aren't you together?"

Such a simple question.

…

What do I tell them?

How am I supposed to say –

KAYLEE AND ADELYN by Elizabeth Shannon

…

Kaylee was always better at talking to people.

Maybe she'd know the right thing to do.

And I don't want to break their hearts

So I almost want to lie

To say it was a joke,

That I am Kaylee.

Maybe they would never figure out the truth.

…

…

…

But

I have to tell them.

That I am

Just.

Adelyn.

…

I still hear her sometimes.

I still see her.

I feel her.

(Adelyn stops, as if waiting for Kaylee to say something. Silence.)

And at her funeral

The casket was closed, it had to be, but…

I saw people looking at me

As if they were imagining me in there

Trying to piece together what it would look like

Or as if they were seeing Kaylee there

Her ghost, her spirit,

Or maybe
Her alive
And they were secretly, silently, wishing that it was
Kaylee
And not Adelyn
Who survived.
…
And my mama still messes it up sometimes
Shouts up the stairs
Starts with …her name
And now it's just
Adelyn.
(Silence.)
And Adelyn.
(Silence.)
And Adelyn.
(Silence.)
And Adelyn.
…
Adelyn.
Adelyn.
(Blackout.)
Adelyn.

END OF PLAY

MADAM TIFFANI, THE MINOR ARCANE

by Michael Lin

Tiffani, a grade school tarot reader, weighs in on the fates and fortunes of Andie and Ducky, two friends who are teetering on the edge of being something more.

CHARACTERS

Madam TIFFANI
she/her, ~7 years old, A precocious young entrepreneur, doing her best to project an aura of mystic wisdom.

DUCKY
any gender [he/him default], 30's-50's, but near in age to Andie. Rational, reserved, and a skeptic.

ANDIE (or ANDY)
any gender [she/her default], 30's-50's, but near in age to Ducky. Warm, vulnerable, and a fan of the mystical.

SETTING

Daytime. A school gymnasium or courtyard full of unseen people.

MADAM TIFFANI, THE MINOR ARCANE by Michael Lin

***

A slapdash kiosk stands center stage, bearing a sign: "TAROT READINGS: 25¢". Nearby are a table with tablecloth and a few places to sit – stools, cushions, folding chairs, upturned LEGO tubs, whatever a child might have pulled to hand. Perhaps some conspicuous battery powered candles on the table for atmosphere, to be "lit" whenever the moment feels right. Madam Tiffani, the child in question, is encamped in the most comfortable seat, eager and attentive for passersby.

Ducky and Andie enter, wearing name tags.

Importantly, their body language indicates friendship, not romance. They're sipping lemonade from small disposable cups.

ANDIE. Look, a little tarot reader! Isn't she cute?

DUCKY. Aww, yeah, she's precious. *(beat)* And maybe a little appropriative, I'm not sure.

ANDIE. Ducky!

DUCKY. No, you're right, that's not her fault, she's just a kid.

ANDIE. Let's get a reading.

DUCKY. Ehhh...

ANDIE. What?

DUCKY. That stuff is a scam, you know.

ANDIE. That's such a Scorpio thing to say.

DUCKY. C'mon...

ANDIE. I know you don't like astrology, but can you at least admit that it's interesting to think about? Just a little? Something to tell you how your day might go, what that dream meant. *(meaningfully)* Who you might be compatible with? Maybe in an "opposites attract" kind of way?

DUCKY. ...yeah, of course. I've thought about that stuff a lot. But that kind of question is too important to me not to at least try to be rational about it. And sometimes – no matter how appealing an idea is – sometimes it just doesn't make sense on paper.

ANDIE. "On paper"?

TIFFANI. *(waving)* Hi!

(Andie and Ducky turn to look.)

Aren't ya gonna come to my booth?

DUCKY. Hi, sweetie, we're still thinking about it. Give us a minute, okay?

TIFFANI. Did ya have to think that hard about Johnny's lemonade stand?

(Tiffani looks significantly at the little cups in Andie and Ducky's hands.)

It's okay, you don't have to come to my stall if you don't wanna. Lots of other kids have cool stuff you can do. And I know it's cuz I'm a girl...

(No matter how obvious the manipulation, the implications of this suggestion are unacceptable. Andie and Ducky rush in and sit in the two remaining places.)

ANDIE. Don't be silly, we would be happy to support a young lady entrepreneur like you. Isn't that right?

DUCKY. Yep, absolutely.

TIFFANI. Yay! That will be twenty-five cents, please.

(Ducky produces the change and places it on the table.)

DUCKY. *(to Andie)* My treat.

(Tiffani. pockets the coin.)

TIFFANI. *(preprepared speech)* Allow me to introduce myself. Ahem.

(Tiffani stands on her seat.)

I am the most arcane of Ms. Beasley's second grade class's small business festival. I am your guide through the mystical waters of your future. I know everything; my mommy says so. I can show you things that were! Things that are! And some stuff that has not yet come to pass!

DUCKY. *(recognizing the "inspiration")* – hey, wait a minute –

ANDIE. Shh!

TIFFANI. I! Am Madam Tiffani! With an "I"! *(imitates sound of crashing thunder)*

(Tiffani resumes her seat.)

And who are you?

DUCKY. *(good humored)* You're the psychic, don't you already know that?

(Andie and Ducky obligingly display their nametags prominently. Tiffani leans in and squints.)

TIFFANI. Nice to meet you ... "Dandy" and "Yucky."

ANDIE. *(gently)* Andie.

DUCKY. Ducky.

TIFFANI. And who shall be receiving this reading?

(Ducky points to Andie immediately.)

ANDIE. Me, please.

(Tiffani draws out a deck of mismatched-looking tarot cards.)

TIFFANI. Lucky you, you're the first ones to try my new special tarot deck!

(Andie nods. Tiffani reverently shuffles the deck, then presents the deck to Andie to cut. She makes a show of displaying her empty sleeves and clean hands, like a Vegas casino dealer. Andie cuts the deck and presents it back to Tiffani, who takes it in hand and draws four

cards from the top for her reading. With each card she reveals, she places it on the table in front of Andie.)

The Sun. It represents warmth, fun, and youthful energy. This is you, your past.

(Another card.)

The Lovers. Love, yes. But also imbalance – harmony and disharmony and dat-harmony. In your present, something is not the way you want it in the realm of love.

(Another card.)

The 10 of Cups. Fullness in your heart, joy, and happiness. This is what lies ahead for you in your future. So long as you can defeat –

(A final card.)

The Magician. The magician solves problems, but using tricks and manipoo – manipuluh...

(Tiffani squints at some writing on the card, put there by her.)

Ma-ni-pu-lay-shun. Overcome this man-i-play-tive nature, and you shall have what you seek.

ANDIE. *(in awe)* Wow... that's amazing.

DUCKY. That was actually fun to watch. Nice hustle, kid.

TIFFANI. You don't believe?

DUCKY. Absolutely not.

ANDIE. *(admonishing)* Ducky!

DUCKY. What? She asked. Like I said, that was a great amount of entertainment for the price. But predicting the future? I don't buy it.

TIFFANI. Maybe a reading of your own would change your mind.

DUCKY. Sorry, I'm out of quarters.

(Andie slams a quarter on the table.)

ANDIE. Please. Allow me.

(Tiffani looks at him expectantly.)

DUCKY. ...sure.

Tiffani gathers up the cards from Andie's spread and shuffles them back into the deck. She follows the same ritual from before, presenting the deck to Ducky to cut. He does so and passes the deck back to Tiffani. With a grand gesture, an attitude of challenge, she begins to draw cards.

TIFFANI. The Knight of Coins. Logical and practical.

ANDIE. Sounds about right.

TIFFANI. Shush...

ANDIE. Oh! Sorry.

TIFFANI. You like stuff to be clear and simple. But that also makes you bored.

(Another card.)

The Two of Swords.

(Ducky sits up and looks at the card closely.)

DUCKY. That's a Pokémon!

TIFFANI. Doublade [duhblade] represents tough decisions. Are you gonna be passive, or active? Communication is powerful, but comes with the risk of discord servers.

(Another card.)

Uno.

DUCKY. What?!

TIFFANI. The Wild Draw-4 is about seizing opportunities. What feels like a step backwards is really just giving you more tools to take your life in a new direction. Think on that.

DUCKY. Uhhuh...

(One final card.)

TIFFANI. And finally... second prize in a beauty contest.

DUCKY. Where did you get these cards?!

TIFFANI. I told you, it's my special deck. *(beat)* Beauty contest. Second prize. You're more desirable than you think you are. Keep your feet on the ground, but... it's okay to know your value. To enter a new situation knowing you can't predict the ending.

DUCKY. What are you trying to pull here?

TIFFANI. What do you mean?

DUCKY. I already told you that I don't buy into this stuff... and I'll be honest, this hasn't really changed my mind. But if you were a pro charging a hundred bucks instead of a quarter, I'd feel cheated! It was nice hanging out, Andie, but I'm going home.

(Ducky gets up to leave. Tiffani climbs atop her chair.)

TIFFANI. STOP!!

(A sudden, booming command, full of Galadriel-esque presence. Ducky stops.)

MISTER YUCKY. YOU NEED NOT BELIEVE TO GLEAN INSIGHT FROM MY WORDS.

DUCKY. ...okay.

TIFFANI. DO YOU HAVE A QUESTION FOR THE UNIVERSE??

DUCKY. ...y-yes.

TIFFANI. LOUDER!

DUCKY. Yes!

TIFFANI. ARE YOU HOLDING IT IN YOUR HEART?!

DUCKY. Yes!

TIFFANI. ARE YOU PREPARED TO ANSWER IT YOURSELF??

DUCKY. YES!

TIFFANI. WITH THE WISDOM I HAVE IMPARTED!?

DUCKY. I AM!!

TIFFANI. THEN WAIT NO LONGER!!

DUCKY. I WON'T!

TIFFANI. TAKE CHANCES!

DUCKY. YES!

TIFFANI. MAKE MISTAKES!!

DUCKY. WHAT?!

TIFFANI. GET MESSY!!

DUCKY. I KNOW WHAT THAT'S FROM, BUT I HEED ANYWAY!!

TIFFANI. TAKE YOUR LEAP OF FAITH, FOOLISH MORTAL!!

DUCKY. OKAY!!

(Ducky pivots to Andie.)

WILL YOU GO OUT WITH ME??

ANDIE. FREAKING FINALLY!!

(Andie leaps up and embraces Ducky with a shared scream of jubilation. Any sound or light cues associated with Tiffani's outburst vanish; we are grounded once again.)

DUCKY. I still don't think our star signs mean anything.

ANDIE. Shush.

(Out of Ducky's view, Andie passes Tiffani a small bundle of cash. Tiffani pockets it and gathers her tarot deck together to prepare for whoever her next client might be.)

END OF PLAY

MISSED DISCONNECTIONS

by Samara Siskind

In the age of swiping left or right, three millennials defy the odds by looking for love the good old-fashioned way... on Craigslist.

CHARACTERS

BEN
Male, early thirties, a hopeless romantic.

SLOAN
Female, late twenties, a girl with her guard up.

MARGOT
Female, mid-twenties, just wants to be noticed.

SETTING

A city park, anywhere.

***

A park bench. A man sits, smiling to himself. Woman enters. He stands.

SLOAN. W4M - 27. We locked eyes for a second this morning at Whole Foods. I was wearing a red polka dotted sundress, you had on jeans and a hipster sport jacket. There was a banana in your basket next to a pint of chocolate milk, like a child's lunch. I thought that was adorable.

BEN. M4W - 32. I noticed you sniffing and fondling half a dozen grapefruits at Whole Foods on 14th. Your red dress and little white sneakers destroyed me. I was the guy with the fogged up glasses in the freezer aisle. I hope you read these things. *(holding out hand)* Ben.

SLOAN. Sloan. *(nervous)* I can't believe I'm doing this.

BEN. First timer?

SLOAN. Missed Connection virgin. I mean, I've written dozens... in my head. This is the first time I've been brave enough to post one. Do people even use this anymore?

BEN. I'm pretty sure it's mostly personals now. But hey, we're here.

SLOAN. Strange, isn't it? I mean, good strange, not freaky strange. Two people posting about each other, *to* each other.

BEN. I looked for you at every checkout lane that day. I circled the parking lot twice, but you disappeared. I was kicking myself for not talking to you.

SLOAN. Why didn't you?

BEN. Let's see. Good old-fashioned fear? Fear of rejection. Fear of a jacked-up boyfriend appearing out of nowhere ... Fear of coming off like a creeper interrupting a magical moment between a girl and her produce. *(beat)* Why did you write to me?

SLOAN. You look like a boy who broke my heart in 6th grade, all grown up. *(beat)* I made a New Year's resolution to be more spontaneous so, I finally threw my message in a bottle into the ocean. Way more romantic than asking someone for their number, right?

BEN. Missed Connections *are* safer than Tinder.

SLOAN. We've already seen each other in the flesh.

BEN. No fear of being cat fished.

SLOAN. The initial spark is already there.

(Beat.)

BEN. You're wearing it, the dress.

SLOAN. I thought I'd make it easy for you to spot me.

BEN. I spotted you in a sea of over a hundred organic food shoppers.

(A few beats. Fleeting glances. Half smiles.)

SLOAN. So, I'm going to hit the coffee cart over there and text my friend that I'm still alive. Would you like a coffee? Chocolate milk?

BEN. No thanks. I just had a Lunchables.

(Sloan smiles and exits, giving him one last head turn. Ben sits as before, pleased. A woman enters. Ben does a double take, then stands.)

(flustered) M4W - 32. You were wearing a short denim skirt and a green shirt with puffy sleeves. You stood next to me in the red wine aisle eating from a bag of chickpea snacks. You looked amazing. I hope you see this.

MARGOT. Hi. Ben? Sorry I'm a little late, I've never been to this park. The layout is confusing. *(reaching her hand out)* Margot.

BEN. Margot. Hi, uh. Wow, you look great! *(looking off)* Weren't we supposed to meet Sunday?

MARGOT. It's not –? Wait.

(Checks her watch.)

Oh no. I'm a day early. Oopsies!

BEN. No, no worries.

MARGOT. Well, since we're already here.

(Plops down.)

I guess subconsciously I wanted it to be tomorrow. Can I just tell you, I like, loved what you wrote. It just made me feel so, like *(fanning herself)* flattered you know? Like, *noticed.* Being admired from afar. I can't stop thinking about it. I didn't even think people used Missed Connections anymore. Don't they use TikTok now? I've never posted, I'm a horrible writer, but I still read it sometimes. I always hoped someone would write to me.

BEN. Well, I'm, I'm, glad it, it did all that. Look, I –

MARGOT. So, did you end up getting the Cab or the Zin?

(Ben just looks at her, confused.)

The wine. Did you end up going for the Cabernet or the Zinfandel?

BEN. Oh, ah, huh. You know, I – I don't remember.

MARGOT. I hope you went with the Zin, it would've gone great with the feta.

BEN. The feta?

MARGOT. In your basket, silly.

BEN. The cheese! Yes! So, uh, you know I think tomorrow would be better.

MARGOT. Better for what?

BEN. For this, this meeting.

MARGOT. Tomorrow? You want me to come back here tomorrow?

BEN. It looks like it's going to rain.

MARGOT. My smartwatch says it's sunny with low chance of showers.

BEN. Yeah, well, I have another... I was headed to my mom's house, actually.

MARGOT. But it took me *(checking watch)* 2,668 steps to get here from my car.

BEN. I'm really sorry. She's old and I need to help her... walk.

(Sloan enters.)

SLOAN. Hi.

BEN. Hey.

MARGOT. Hi.

(Painfully awkward silence. Finally –)

SLOAN. I'm sorry. Am I interrupting something?

MARGOT. *(blissfully unaware)* It's our first date. Missed Connection at Whole Foods. He liked my puffy sleeved top. Isn't that romantic? *(to Sloan)* You look familiar. Do you two know each other?

SLOAN. Really? You double booked a Missed Connection?

BEN. No, no!

SLOAN. I can't believe this. You're, you're, my ex! You're Mason Mayfield all over again!

BEN. Sloan, I – Let me –

SLOAN. My first middle school dance. My first date, ever! I go to get some punch and BAM! There he is making out with Shari Snipes behind the DJ table. You even look like him!

MARGOT. I got the day wrong. We're supposed to meet tomorrow. Ooohhh. That's why you wanted me to go.

SLOAN. He wanted you to go?

MARGOT. To come back tomorrow. He said he needed to

help his mom... walk.

SLOAN. Okay, wow. I knew I shouldn't have come. Just when I finally find an ounce of courage to put myself out there.

BEN. Please, can I just –

SLOAN. It's all about the chase for you, isn't it? You find it entertaining to manipulate women's feelings?! Lead them on and, and lie to them?!

BEN. No! I don't! I didn't lie, or lead anyone on! I met you after I met ah, ah –

MARGOT. Margot.

BEN. Margot, right!

SLOAN. And then you wanted to ditch her?!

BEN. I didn't want to ditch her! I just wanted to see her tomorrow. As planned.

SLOAN. Unbelievable.

BEN. What's unbelievable? I never said it was my first time posting. I never said it was my only time. Did you know men on average fall in love 19 times a day?

MARGOT. I believe the statistic is men think about sex 19 times a day.

SLOAN. Does this mean 17 other women are going to show up?

BEN. It means I've thrown a lot of bottles into the ocean.

MARGOT. That's not very eco-conscious, Ben.

BEN. So, what? I'm not allowed to have two dates in the same weekend?

SLOAN. It's not that. It's you approaching both of us in the same exact way. Me in my red dress, her in her puff sleeves. Like, like a formula. Sending us these parallel posts cheapens it all. It's the equivalent of rotating the same pick-up line at a bar.

BEN. Well, it's hard for guys too! I don't do this just to hook up. None of these things have ever worked out for me. Like the cute Uber driver who ended up stealing the silverware from my favorite diner. Or the flirty bank teller whose entire Instagram account was pictures of her cat wearing doll clothes. There's more.

SLOAN. Oh cry me a river. You just didn't want to put all of y our Whole Food eggs in one basket.

BEN. Well, what about you?

SLOAN. Me?! What about me?

BEN. At least I try! Fine, maybe I try too often, but you don't try at all!

SLOAN. You don't know anything about me!

BEN. I know that Mason Mayfield guy sure did a number on you. I know you don't take chances. You bury moments that could turn into something beautiful. You sit on the sidelines instead of throwing your hat in the ring.

SLOAN. Yeah, except for this time! And look what happened!

BEN. Look, let's just take a moment. *(beat)* I, I saw...

(Lost. Looks at Margot for help.)

MARGOT. Margot.

BEN. Margot. I saw Margot and took a shot in the dark. Most people don't even know the Missed Connections section of craigslist exists. She responded. We made plans. Then saw you with the grapefruits, so I took another shot in the dark. Then *you* posted to *me*! How amazing is that? What was I supposed to do?

SLOAN. You could have changed locations.

MARGOT. At least he picked different days.

BEN. Look, my only crime here, if it can even be considered a crime, is finding the both of you attractive and seeing potential for something more. You'll never win the lottery unless you buy a ticket. *(beat)* Or multiple tickets.

(Sloan turns to Margot.)

SLOAN. How do you feel about all this?

MARGOT. We only have one life. I think Ben was just being realistic about his needs and accepting that a moment of intimacy between two strangers doesn't always evolve into a deep, long-lasting connection. It's hit or miss, and timing is everything. If I hadn't shown up you two might be seeing a movie together or making plans for dinner. He hasn't forgotten your name.

BEN. Sorry about that.

MARGOT. You remembered Mason Mayfield.

SLOAN. So you think he deserves a second chance?

MARGOT. No.

BEN. No?

MARGOT. After scrolling my smartwatch, I see a few more trademark Ben Whole Foods posts and two at Trader Joe's, which leads me to believe... you're just a serial poster.

(Shrugs.)

Sorry Ben. *(beat)* Wait. Did I just feel a drop? *(looking up)* Oh no! My smartwatch said no rain!

(Margot reaches into her bag for an umbrella. As she takes her umbrella out, a hat falls to the ground. Sloan and Margot both reach down to pick it up and lock eyes.)

(Beat.)

SLOAN. W4W - 27. Cute girl in the yellow bucket hat. We reached for the same copy of Franny and Zooey at Second Chance Books. You let me have it. I love your smile and the star tattoos on your wrist.

(Margot holds up her wrist, revealing her stars.)

MARGOT. You wrote that? About me? I never saw it.

SLOAN. I never sent it. I wrote it ... in my head.

MARGOT. You were wearing cat-eye glasses and had a reusable farmer's market tote with a whole wheat baguette in it. I knew you looked familiar.

(They slowly stand.)

SLOAN. Thanks again, for the book.

MARGOT. You're welcome.

(A few beats.)

BEN. Well, this is an exciting turn of events. *(hopeful)* Maybe the three of us can find a nice spot for brunch?

SLOAN. It's not happening Ben.

MARGOT. I think you need a time-out.

SLOAN. Do yourself a favor. Find a new venue.

(Margot holds her palm out to the sky, looking up.)

MARGOT

False alarm. *(gestures to Sloan's coffee)* Would you like a refill?

SLOAN. I'd love one.

(Sloan and Margot exit, together. Ben sighs and returns to bench. He takes out his phone and makes a call.)

BEN. Hi there, beautiful. I'm at the park. Want some company? ... Okay, great. I'll see you in a few, Mom.

END OF PLAY

SNACKS, DRUGS, AND THE SEXUAL APPETITES OF THE GAYS

by Steven G. Martin

Newlyweds Aiden and Jake are glad to have time to themselves as their wedding day concludes. But helicopter parents Cathleen and Merle intervene to make sure their little man Aiden is all set for losing his virginity.

CHARACTERS

AIDEN
> *Male. Early-to-mid-20s. Any background. Jake's newlywed husband. Merle and Cathleen's son. Gwen's grandson-in-law.*

JAKE
> *Male. Early-to-mid-20s. Any background. Aiden's newlywed husband. Merle and Cathleen's son-in-law. Gwen's grandson.*

MERLE
> *Male. Late 40s. Any background. Aiden's father. Cathleen's husband. Jake's father-in-law.*

CATHLEEN
> *Female. Late 40s. Any background. Aiden's mother. Merle's wife. Jake's mother-in-law.*

GWEN
> *Female. Late 60s. Any background. Jake's grand mother.*

SETTING

The bedroom in Aiden and Jake's honeymoon suite. A bed with a headboard, or some theater blocks, would suffice. It should be large enough for an actor to hide behind comfortably.

TIME

Late evening after Aiden and Jake's wedding and reception.

** THIS PLAY CONTAINS ADULT LANGUAGE AND THEMES.*

***

At rise, Aiden and Jake kiss.
LIGHTS UP.
Aiden and Jake break the kiss. They hold each other.

JAKE. I have been waiting all day for this.

AIDEN. Dressing up. Driving to the church. Saying vows. Exchanging rings. "You can kiss the groom."

JAKE. Having you to myself.

AIDEN. Photographs. Driving to the reception. Your brother's lousy toast. First dance. Second dance.

JAKE. Getting away from it all. Getting away from your parents.

AIDEN. All the food, all the … What?

JAKE. You know how they're always around, hovering.

AIDEN. Well, they paid for everything, so…

JAKE. I'm sorry. You're right. They're very generous.

AIDEN. *(smiling)* Yes, they are.

JAKE. But no more talk about anyone else. There's only one person I'm thinking of now.

AIDEN. *(big grin)* Who, me?

(Jake nods.)

Well don't I feel special. And now I'm going to make you feel special.

(Aiden gently pushes Jake onto the bed. Jake grins. As Aiden sings, he does a strip tease, revealing light blue boxers.)

"Happy Wedding Night to you. Happy Wedding Night to you. Happy Wedding Night, Mr. Anthropolous-Pescatore. Happy Wedding Night to you." I learned that just for you.

JAKE. *(smiling)* I don't get the reference, and I don't care.

(Cathleen barges in with a tackle box.)

CATHLEEN. It's Marilyn Monroe seducing President Kennedy. You need to be breathier, Aiden.

AIDEN. *(covering up, overlapping)* Mom!

JAKE. *(overlapping)* Mrs. Anthropolous!

CATHLEEN. *(singing à la Marilyn Monroe)* "Happy birthday, Mr. President." Your father loves when I do that. *(She grins.)* Do you like the boxers, Jake? Now you've got "something blue"! Don't worry, they aren't old or borrowed.

AIDEN. Mom, get *out!*

CATHLEEN. *(to Jake)* He always says that when I interrupt him *in flagrante delicto.* Oh, and I see Marilyn worked!

(Cathleen pats Jake's shoulder lightly and winks.)

JAKE. Mrs. Anthropolous, please! It's been a long day and Aiden and I … want to rest.

CATHLEEN. *(instantly concerned)* Why are you tired? You're young. Are you sick? Do you have a fever?

AIDEN. I'm not sick!

CATHLEEN. It must be your blood sugar. You ate nothing all night. You're going to wear yourself out.

AIDEN. No, Mom. I'm not hungry.

CATHLEEN. I have just the thing.

(Cathleen opens the tackle box.)

It's a snackle box. You know, a tackle box with snacks. Patty Durkster saw it on Food Network's "Mary Makes It Easy." I loaded it with sweet and salty goodies. Tell me what you want.

JAKE. He isn't hungry, Mrs. Anthropolous.

CATHLEEN. *(staring hard at Jake)* I think I know my own son. *(To Aiden)* I've got M&M's, potato chips, even Twinkies.

(Merle enters with a thick, three-ring binder with colored tabs.)

MERLE. Twinkies is an offensive term, Cathleen. The Gays prefer "femmes," isn't that right, son?

AIDEN. *(overlapping)* Dad!

JAKE. *(overlapping)* Mr. Anthropolous!

MERLE. Not that my son is a femme. Remember that other term? Otter? Trim, defined build, a little hairy. Playful. But they must not like swimming or Slip 'N Slides. Water Sports was its own category.

AIDEN. *(sitting next to Jake)* This is a nightmare. Pinch me.

(Jake pinches Aiden's arm.)

Ow!

JAKE. Why are you here?

CATHLEEN. It's Aiden's big night. We've always been there for him. Throwing birthday parties.

MERLE. Chaperoning class trips.

CATHLEEN. Standing up to teachers.

MERLE. Standing up to coaches.

CATHLEEN. Earning Boy Scout merit badges.

MERLE. Completing homework *and doing it right*. Math. History.

CATHLEEN. Driver's ed. Phys ed. We've always supported our little man.

MERLE. Even tonight, when he's preparing to lose his virginity.

JAKE. Um –

CATHLEEN. He would have failed sex ed without us. He wanted to put his pee-pee in such odd places.

MERLE. I think The Gays prefer the term "cock," dear. Isn't that right, boys?

CATHLEEN. Ugh! "Cock." That makes me think of roosters, which makes me think of Foghorn Leghorn.

(à la Porky Pig)

Th-th-th-th-that's all folks!

AIDEN. Mom, that's Porky Pig.

CATHLEEN. Don't contradict your mother. Ugh! "Pork." We're doing this for you, you know.

MERLE. Your first time should be special. And since it won't make a baby, you might as well have fun.

CATHLEEN. And you did almost fail sex ed, in spite of how much you masturbated. Gallons, Jake. Gallons.

AIDEN. I am praying for a sinkhole to swallow the hotel.

JAKE. Pray harder.

MERLE. *(raising the three-ring binder)* Your mother and I conducted research to make sure you're prepared for every possibility.

AIDEN. You didn't have to, I –

CATHLEEN. *(sweetly passive-aggressive)* Well, what else was I going to do with all my time? Knit baby booties for the dozens of grandchildren you're going to give me?

MERLE / AIDEN / JAKE. Ouch.

CATHLEEN. *Anyway.* We conducted research.

AIDEN. How?

JAKE. Don't tell us!

MERLE. We looked at all the gay pornography we could find. Books.

CATHLEEN. Magazines.

MERLE. Internet. There was a surprising amount of pornography for The Gays.

CATHLEEN. We learned all we could.

MERLE. And we're going to pass it onto you, son.

(*Merle holds up the three-ring binder.*)

It's color-coded. I know you're a visual learner.

CATHLEEN. But first: Are you a top or a bottom?

JAKE. Where did you learn those words?

MERLE. They're everywhere, Jake. PornHub, ThePorn Dude, Porn.com, PornGeek, PornMate, PornMD, The Lord of Porn, xHamster, XVideos, XNXX, RedTube, SparkBang, and Saturday Night Live.

CATHLEEN. So? Top or bottom?

MERLE. Now, Cathleen, don't pressure the boy. Maybe he's neither. Maybe he's a side.

AIDEN. *(overlap)* Please, no.

CATHLEEN. *(overlap)* What's a side?

JAKE. *(overlap)* Aiden don't say a word.

MERLE. A side doesn't like to…

(*Merle swallows hard in discomfort.*)

…baste the inside of a turkey. Or have the inside of his turkey basted.

AIDEN. Dad, you're ruining Thanksgiving.

MERLE. *(referring to a page in the binder)* They prefer to kiss or cuddle. They like mutual masturbation, frottage, rimming, pit play, nip play, muscle worship, docking (if they're uncut). Activities that don't require … basting.

CATHLEEN. Merle, if you mean penetration then "basting" is the wrong word. Basting means to pour liquid over meat to keep it moist. A better choice would be "packing the turkey's cavity with stuffing."

MERLE. But isn't that fisting?

JAKE. What is happening?!

AIDEN. How did you learn all this?

MERLE. I conducted online interviews. There's a very popular website called Gay dot U-S.

(Jake freezes, then stares at Merle.)

Some very nice Gays, and even some Bi's, shared information.

CATHLEEN. Bless their little pink hearts.

MERLE. You wouldn't believe how many responded when I wrote that I was a married man looking to help my son.

(Merle refers to the three-ring binder.)

There was BamBam and JJxDadStallion. BDGF and RSJM. HairyNWet, Jackhammer47, LikeItRough, Hard Starter, Muscleman360, HockeyBrat, Jock2Pervert, CuriousJock. All of them like BBC; I didn't know British TV was so popular. RedneckSkater, NotSo Straight, BiMarriedGuy, BalkanBiDad, HungSpeedo Dad, Head4Men, TexCattleMan, MuscleControlled, ParkPig, XTremePig666, ILoveOlderMen –

(Jake coughs.)

– Cowboy4U, NoGag, and SmallPouch. You can have pride no matter your size, son.

JAKE. *(nonchalantly)* What was your username, Mr.

Anthropolous?

MERLE. I said already: MarriedDadForSon.

(Jake coughs and blusters. Only Aiden notices, who glares and knows.)

You should have that cough checked out, Jake.

AIDEN. *(pointedly)* I'll take care of him.

CATHLEEN. *(oblivious)* What a good boy. But let's take care of you now. Do you need snacks?

AIDEN. No, Mom.

MERLE. How about Viagra? You know, the little blue pill? Keeps me hard as timber, boys.

CATHLEEN. It works. I nearly dislocated my jaw.

AIDEN. Mom, I don't want pills for sex. I don't need them, and I don't trust them.

CATHLEEN. But I've wrapped one in a fruit roll-up.

(Cathleen shows it to Aiden to tempt him.)

Your favorite: Jolly Rancher Green Apple.

AIDEN. Awww.

CATHLEEN. *(surreptitiously)* I've also got cannabis gummies if that'll get you in the mood.

AIDEN. Mom!

MERLE. Son, please don't be mad. We just want your first time to be special.

CATHLEEN. Losing your virginity is … well, it's cliché but true. You never forget your first.

(Jake coughs demonstrably.)

You really should see a doctor about that cough, Jake.

JAKE. I'm sorry, I really am. But Aiden is not a virgin. He does not need you to make this night special with snacks or drugs or research into sexual appetites of The Gays. The striptease and singing worked nicely, thank you, but no more. Please let us enjoy our wedding night alone.

CATHLEEN. *(to Aiden, shocked)* Not a virgin?

AIDEN. *(shrugging)* No.

MERLE. Son, have you basted?

AIDEN. Dad …

MERLE. Sorry, "packed."

AIDEN. Dad!

MERLE. Sorry. Sorry.

CATHLEEN. Well, our little man doesn't need us anymore, Merle. I am surprised. I am hurt. I wish I had known this before we *haggled with Days Inn for 30 percent off the rooms for the wedding party.*

MERLE. He's a grown man, dear. But he'll always be our boy. And I'll always be your father.

AIDEN. Thanks, Dad.

MERLE. And he's got a great man in his life, whom I'll love like a son. I hope you'll also call me Dad.

JAKE. Not a chance.

CATHLEEN. There's nothing to do, then, except leave so they can enjoy their wedding night. Good night.

AIDEN / JAKE. Good night.

(Cathleen and Merle start to exit with the snackle box and three-ring binder, when:)

AIDEN. Hey Mom, can you leave the snackle box? I probably could have something to eat.

CATHLEEN. Of course!

(Cathleen rushes to Aiden to hand him the snackle box.)

Good night.

AIDEN / JAKE. Good night.

(Cathleen and Merle start to leave.)

AIDEN. Dad, could you leave the research? I'm not a virgin, but that doesn't mean I can't learn something new.

MERLE. Of course!

(Merle rushes to Aiden to hand him the three-ring binder.)

Good night.

AIDEN / JAKE. Good night.

(Cathleen and Merle start to leave.)

AIDEN. Can I have fifty bucks?

(Merle rushes to Aiden to hand him a $100 bill.)

MERLE. Here's a hundred. Keep it.

AIDEN. Aww. Thanks, Dad.

(Merle nods. He and Cathleen smile and exit. Aiden closes the door.)

JAKE. Hover. They hover so much.

(Aiden waves the bill at Jake.)

Which isn't always a bad thing.

AIDEN. *(as he nods)* You are deleting your account from that website tonight.

JAKE. Way ahead of you.

(Gwen, Jake's grandmother, springs up from behind the bed where she was hiding from the beginning of the play.)

GWEN. Finally, they're gone! Hi, Baby Jakey!

JAKE. Grandma?!

END OF PLAY

STEPHEN HAWKING'S TRAIN

by Mike Byham

On 28 June 2009, British astrophysicist Stephen Hawking hosted a party for time travelers in the University of Cambridge. Professor Hawking did not send out the invitations until the following day, after the party was over. In preparing for the event, Hawking said he hoped that copies of the invite might survive for thousands of years, and that "one day someone living in the future will find the information and use a wormhole time machine to come back to my party, proving that time travel will one day be possible." Hawking reportedly waited in the room for a few hours before leaving, and no visitors arrived. He stated that the event was "experimental evidence that time travel is not possible". But was he truthful?

CHARACTERS

PERSON 1
> *Train passenger, any gender, any age.*

PERSON 2
> *Time traveler, any gender, any age.*

PERSON 3
> *Another time traveler, any gender, any age.*

SETTING

The morning of June 28th, 2009, on a train from London to Cambridge.

***

Lights up on Person 1 seated on a train, reading a newspaper. The train goes through a tunnel and lights flicker off, then back on. During the time the lights were off, Person 2 appears in the seat next to Person 1 - as if he simply appeared out of thin air.

PERSON 1. Oh! Hello.

PERSON 2. Greetings.

(Person 2 grins, looking around train in wonder.)

Is this the train to fifty-two degrees, twelve minutes, twenty-one seconds north, seven degrees, seven minutes, four point seven seconds east?

PERSON 1. I'm sorry?

PERSON 2. Yes. Which train am I on?

PERSON 1. This is the Great Northern to Cambridge.

PERSON 2. Cambridge. Excellent.

(Person 1 nods to himself and returns to the newspaper.)

Please pardon me once again. This is the morning of the twenty-eighth of June in two-thousand and nine, Anno Domini?

PERSON 1. *(showing the date on the newspaper)* That's what it says here.

PERSON 2. Excellent.

(Person 1 returns to reading. Person 2 giggles, getting louder until Person 1 lowers the newspaper and stares at Person 2)

PERSON 1. What's so funny?

PERSON 2. Oh, you wouldn't believe me.

PERSON 1. No?

PERSON 2. I can hardly believe it, myself. But this ... this train ... and you ... are proof! I've done it!

PERSON 1. Done what?

PERSON 2. The impossible.

PERSON 1. Well, that can't be true.

PERSON 2. It can't?

PERSON 1. By definition. If you do the impossible, it never was impossible, right?

PERSON 2. Ah. Of course. Let me rephrase. I did something that was thought impossible.

PERSON 1. Better.

(Beat as Person 2 just grins at Person 1.)

So, are you going to tell me?

PERSON 2. You won't believe me.

PERSON 1. Try me.

PERSON 2. Well, okay then. *(beat)* I'm a time traveler.

PERSON 1. Time traveler?

PERSON 2. Yes.

PERSON 1. Aren't we all? Aren't we all just traveling through time?

PERSON 2. Can you travel backwards? To the past?

PERSON 1. I see. You're from the future then?

PERSON 2. I am! Many years – centuries in fact! And I am the first to travel back in time.

PERSON 1. Hmm.

PERSON 2. You're not impressed?!

PERSON 1. I'm dubious.

PERSON 2. Well, after the party, you'll see. You'll believe me.

PERSON 1. Party?

(Person 2 pulls out a sheet of paper from his pocket.)

PERSON 2. *(reading)* "You are cordially invited to a reception for Time Travelers, hosted by Professor Stephen Hawking. To be held at The University of Cambridge. Address: fifty-two degrees, twelve minutes, twenty-one seconds North, zero degrees, seven minutes, four-point seven seconds East at twelve-hundred Universal Time on the twenty-eighth of June, two thousand and nine."

(Person 2 holds paper up to show Person 1.)

This invitation will not be made public until tomorrow. Therefore, the only way one can even know of the party to attend is to travel back in time. As I have.

PERSON 1. I see. This Professor Hawking is quite clever, isn't he?

PERSON 2. He thinks he can prove that time travel is impossible through use of this experimental exercise. A carnival trick. Won't he be stunned?

PERSON 1. Hmm.

PERSON 2. Yes? What is it now?

PERSON 1. Well, it seemed like you were mildly surprised – pleased but surprised nonetheless – when you discovered where and when you are. Why didn't you know absolutely that you would succeed? You didn't see evidence of past success in your future?

PERSON 2. It is reported that no time traveler appeared at the party. Which leads me to accept one of three conclusions. The first is that time travel is indeed impossible. I have just proven that is not the case. The second is that I missed on my calculations and arrived at the wrong date, time or location. I apparently have correctly calculated what was needed for my journey so that leads me to the only conclusion possible. I have created a new timeline and my old timeline, remaining intact, does not have a successful time traveler attending the party.

PERSON 1. Well, it certainly sounds like you got it all figured out.

PERSON 2. There have been others that tried, you know. But in my timeline, they've not been successful.

PERSON 1. You wouldn't know if they were successful though, would you? They would create a new timeline.

PERSON 2. Alas, you are correct. Yet, in this timeline I will be a hero. The genius arriving from a glittering future bringing secrets of science that will shortcut humanity's advancement. It won't be long until we're seeding the galaxy, disease forgotten, life spans extended twice over. It will be a time of wonder and excitement. Brought about by yours truly.

PERSON 1. How exciting.

PERSON 2. It is, isn't it?

PERSON 1. And yet ...

PERSON 2. Yes?

PERSON 1. Perhaps you didn't think of all possible outcomes. Maybe you never make it to the party.

PERSON 2. Yes, yes, I've thought of that. If that is the case and we are working with a single timeline, there would be news of my demise – an accident of note. I've researched this possibility and found that this train – the very train we're currently on – does in fact arrive at Cambridge Station as scheduled.

PERSON 1. But no mention of a time traveler disembarking?

PERSON 2. Again – not in my timeline.

PERSON 1. That's right. Multiple timelines.

PERSON 2. You see, it's pretty solid. I have done it.

PERSON 1. Well, congratulations then.

PERSON 2. And to you as well. You know, as the first

person to meet me here on this train, you will be famous too!

PERSON 1. That's not what I'm interested in. I'd prefer to just stay in the background and do what I do.

PERSON 2. Fame holds no allure?

PERSON 1. None.

PERSON 2. Do you have a cause celebre? Is there something you believe in? Something that will benefit from having a world-wide platform? This is an opportunity you shouldn't ignore. This benefit of the fame I can bring you should be used, not wasted. What cause do you support? There must be something!

PERSON 1. Well, now that you mention it, there is something that I support.

PERSON 2. See? That's what I'm talking about.

PERSON 1. The thing is ... world-wide exposure is the very last thing that would benefit my interest.

PERSON 2. Intriguing. A secret?

PERSON 1. Yes.

PERSON 2. Can you share this secret with me?

PERSON 1. Certainly. The secret is you.

PERSON 2. Is me? But I won't be a secret for long, though, will I?

PERSON 1. Oh no, you will be. A forever secret, I'm afraid. You and all the others.

PERSON 2. Others?

PERSON 1. I believe in keeping the timeline as is.

(Person 1 stands and pulls a gunlike weapon from the inside of his jacket. He shows it to Person 2.)

PERSON 2. That looks like a molecular disruptor! Where did you get that? That's impossible! A molecular disruptor!

PERSON 1. Is it though? Hmm, I suppose it is.

PERSON 2. Where are you from?

PERSON 1. Don't you mean when?

PESRON 2 I don't understand. You ... you are a time traveler too?

PERSON 1. I'm the original time traveler. I arrived a year ago, got to know the time period, the politics, the social scene, made new friends ...

PERSON 2. But ...

PERSON 1. ... and my good friend Stephen and I believe preserving this timeline is what's best. I'm so sorry.

PERSON 2. You're not sorry. You're pathetic! You have done something great. Something momentous. You have traveled through time to a period rife with possibility. You could be the catalyst accelerating humanity's rise, elevating these savages to their rightful destiny – a place of enlightenment. In return, you could be rich. You could be famous. You could be king. A god among men! Instead, you partner with this ... this intellectual hack to maintain this glacial pace of advancement! No, you're not sorry. That's too small a word. You're not sorry.

PERSON 1. I guess I'm not at that. Goodbye, almost famous.

(Train goes through a tunnel. Lights go down and come back up with Person 1 seated once again reading the newspaper. Person 3 Appears seated next to Person 1 looking around in wonder.)

PERSON 3. Hello! Is this the train to Cambridge?

PERSON 1. Yes. Yes, it is.

PERSON 3. I did it!

PERSON 1. Congratulations.

END OF PLAY

THE DIARY OF MARIA

by Dave Huber

After the school play, Maria knows her dad is not coming to pick her up and Maria's director, Mr. Harris, must decide if he can do what any decent person would do.

CHARACTERS

MARIA
> *17, F, High school senior.*

MR. HARRIS
> *37, M, High school drama teacher.*

SETTING

The present. 11:00 PM. Sidewalk outside a high school two hours after the school play.

***

At rise, Maria is sitting on a bench writing in a journal. Mr. Harris sees her and walks to her.

MR. HARRIS. I thought you'd be gone long ago.

MARIA. I was waiting for my dad to pick me up.

MR. HARRIS. The play ended two hours ago. Did he forget about you?

MARIA. No. He had something come up … an emergency.

MR. HARRIS. Well I can't just leave you here to be kidnapped.

MARIA. Don't worry, I'll be fine. I have a lot of writing to do anyway.

MR. HARRIS. No, no, I'll wait with you.

MARIA. Thanks, but I'm safe here. I promise I won't jump into the first car that gives me candy.

MR. HARRIS. Sounds like you were trained well.

MARIA. I was, you can go.

MR. HARRIS. No, no, I'm responsible for you.

MARIA. Were you watching everyone else get picked up tonight?

MR. HARRIS. Well, no but –

MARIA. So, just imagine that you never saw me and assume I got picked up.

MR. HARRIS. Let me just keep you company until he shows up.

MARIA. Please, Mr. Harris, your wife is waiting for you. My dad might be a while.

MR. HARRIS. My wife never waits up for me the night of a play. I'm never home before midnight.

(Maria looks at her phone and answers a call.)

MARIA. It's my dad. Hey Dad … okay great. I'm right in front of the school. Okay.

(She hangs up.)

He'll be here in a minute, you don't have to wait anymore.

MR. HARRIS. I got to talk to him a couple of times on opening night. He was really proud of you.

MARIA. Yeah, he really liked Christine, she was his favorite, and the ending with Michael. He really liked that.

MR. HARRIS. I'm sure you were his favorite.

MARIA. Besides me.

MR. HARRIS. He told me how excited he was to come again tonight. I'm sorry he couldn't make it.

MARIA. The emergency.

MR. HARRIS. I'm glad he enjoyed it. Before the play he told me that he wasn't a big fan of dramas. He was really hoping it was going to be funny.

MARIA. He's pretty emotional and he just doesn't like to cry in front of strangers.

MR. HARRIS. Is that why he sat in the back?

MARIA. Yeah. He cried when we were all taken away at the end. I saw him wiping tears when we walked past him.

MR. HARRIS. That part gets me every time. *(beat)* He told me you were interested in going to college for acting. Is this new?

MARIA. It was just a thought. I don't think so now.

MR. HARRIS. You changed your mind since yesterday?

MARIA. I don't think I'm going to college.

MR. HARRIS. Why not? Your grades are good and there are lots of scholarships out there and community college is practically free.

MARIA. You don't have to wait. He'll be here soon.

MR. HARRIS. It's no problem at all, I'd love to tell him how well you did tonight.

(Maria looks at her phone and answers a call.)

MARIA. Sorry, it's my dad again. Where are ya? … Okay … Okay … Mr. Harris is here waiting with me … Okay … I'll be here.

(She hangs up.)

He'll be here soon and he said for you to go. That you don't have to wait anymore.

MR. HARRIS. He said that?

MARIA. Yeah. So, um, you can go. Don't worry, I'll be fine.

MR. HARRIS. So I'm free to go then?

MARIA. Yep.

MR. HARRIS. I think I'll just wait with you for a few more minutes then I'll go.

MARIA. Please don't.

MR. HARRIS. What's going on?

MARIA. Nothing, I just don't want you to waste your time.

MR. HARRIS. You're usually a pretty good actress, but the phone call was not very convincing.

MARIA. What are you talking about? That was my dad I was talking to.

MR. HARRIS. Nope.

MARIA. Are you saying I'm lying to you? Mr. Harris, I wouldn't lie to you.

MR. HARRIS. Maria … Stop. I know it wasn't your dad on the phone, because you weren't talking to anyone on the phone. Your phone didn't light up when you pretended to take the call. I'm a teacher, I have all kinds of superpowers when it comes to teens and their phones.

MARIA. I'm sorry. He's going to be a while and I didn't

want you to have to wait.

MR. HARRIS. Come on, it'll give us time to chat.

MARIA. Okay … I guess.

MR. HARRIS. Your dad told me that you've wanted to be an actress since you were five.

MARIA. Yeah.

MR. HARRIS. College is a great place to get trained and gain experience.

MARIA. That was the plan.

MR. HARRIS. Something changed that plan?

MARIA. I think so. I think a lot's changed.

MR. HARRIS. Do you still want to act?

MARIA. I do, but –

MR. HARRIS. Tell me why. Why do you love acting?

MARIA. Well … I love to feel someone else's feelings and be in someone else's story. It's like I become more of a person.

MR. HARRIS. More of a person … I like that.

MARIA. I even started my first diary on the day you cast the show.

MR. HARRIS. Really? Is that your diary.

MARIA. It is. It's not a very exciting read right now, but I have a lot to write about from the last two days.

MR. HARRIS. I bet. Opening night was pretty eventful and tonight with Spencer forgetting his lines. You covered those really well.

MARIA. Thanks.

MR. HARRIS. Two more shows to go. I'm sure it'll get a lot more interesting.

MARIA. You've acted before, right?

MR. HARRIS. I have. I know what you mean by becoming

more of a person.

MARIA. Do you get the same feeling when you direct a play? Like, do you feel what Mr Frank feels? Does he become part of you?

MR. HARRIS. I do. Not as much as the actors of course, but yes. Even Anne will always be a small part of me.

MARIA. How many plays have you directed?

MR. HARRIS. Almost a hundred.

MARIA. Wow, that's a lot of small parts in there.

MR. HARRIS. It's getting a little crowded.

MARIA. That's a lot of empathy.

MR. HARRIS. Like I've told you, that's what the arts do best.

MARIA. So, with all that empathy, do you think you would have hidden a Jewish family in your attic?

MR. HARRIS. I'd like to think I would. I hope I'd have the courage to do the right thing.

MARIA. Yeah, me too. Did you know that Miep Gies never thought of herself as a hero. She said "I did what any decent person would have done."

MR. HARRIS. You really did your research.

MARIA. I learned more about World War Two by doing this play and all the research than anything Ms. Jackson ever taught us.

MR. HARRIS. Did you know that Mr. Kraler went to a concentration camp for hiding Anne and her family.

MARIA. And he escaped.

MR. HARRIS. That's right, he did.

MARIA. Mr. Harris … My dad's not coming.

MR. HARRIS. How do you know that?

MARIA. I can't go back home.

MR. HARRIS. What's going on Maria? Come on, tell me the

truth.

MARIA. You sure?

MR. HARRIS. I'm sure. Just know that I'm a mandated reporter. I have to report any abuse you tell me about.

MARIA. Whoa, Mr. Harris, my dad is not abusing me! It's nothing like that.

MR. HARRIS. Well, I'm glad to hear that.

MARIA. It's a lot worse.

MR. HARRIS. Worse?

MARIA. Mr Harris …

MR. HARRIS. Are you sure I'm the one you want to tell?

MARIA. I just know there's a lot of people in this town that I would never tell this to.

MR. HARRIS. What about your dad?

MARIA. Oh, he knows.

MR. HARRIS. And he supports you?

MARIA. Mr Harris … Stop trying to guess what I'm about to tell you … I'm not gay.

MR. HARRIS. Okay, sorry.

MARIA. You said there's a little bit of Anne inside you. I'm really counting on that right now. My dad didn't come to the play tonight. He was going to bring my brother. They were excited. When he didn't show up, I called him at intermission. I called my brother. I called my grandma. No one answered. I walked home after the play. There were flowers on the ground next to our car. They were for me, for the performance tonight. He always brought flowers. They were on their way to see me in the show.

MR. HARRIS. What happened?

MARIA. I won't be at school tomorrow, but I will be there for the play. I just have to find somewhere to go tonight.

MR. HARRIS. To go? Not home?

MARIA. You said … you'd like to think you would hide a family. *(beat)* My dad is undocumented … My grandma is undocumented … My younger brother is undocumented … And I need a place to hide. Just for a little while.

MR. HARRIS. That's … I'm so sorry … I can't believe they just took them.

MARIA. I can't go back home, they must be looking for me.

MR. HARRIS. Your family?

MARIA. No. *(beat)* Mr. Harris, can you help me?

MR. HARRIS. I can call someone for you.

MARIA. Who do you think you're going to call that's going to do the right thing?

MR. HARRIS. Do you have any friends or other family that would put you up for a few days?

MARIA. We don't have any family here, and you're the one adult I trust in this town.

MR. HARRIS. Yeah … um, let me call my wife and tell her what's happening? See what we can do.

(He calls his wife.)

Hi, I know it's late but it's a bit of an emergency. My student Maria, she played Mrs. Frank … yeah, that's her, she needs to stay at our house for a while … yeah, her family was just deported, or detained, and she has nowhere to go … right … I know … yeah, pretty horrible … oh, right … right … that's okay, we'll figure something out … Okay, see ya soon.

(Hangs up.)

MARIA. That's a no, right?

MR. HARRIS. We only have one extra room that's available and it's filled with our living room furniture. We had a leak in a wall and now it all needs to be repainted. So, there's nowhere to put you.

MARIA. You have an attic?

MR. HARRIS. I wouldn't put you in the attic.

MARIA. No, I guess you wouldn't. Maybe you can just make that phone call you were going to make earlier.

MR. HARRIS. I'm sure that child protective services can help find you a place. Let me find the number. I'll stay here and wait with you until someone comes to pick you up. Here it is.

(Calls the number.)

MARIA. Your phone lit up.

MR. HARRIS. What?

MARIA. Just now, your phone lit up your face. Now I see what you were talking about - the superpower.

MR. HARRIS. Oh, right.

MARIA. When you called your wife it didn't light up. I'm sorry Mr Harris, this was a lot to ask of you. I suppose you did what any decent person would have done. Look, I'm just going to my cousin's house. It's just around the corner. I'll see ya, Mr Harris.

(Maria quickly walks away, leaving her diary behind. Mr. Harris watches her leave. He sees the diary and picks it up.)

END OF PLAY

WHEN I SORROW MOST

by Amy Patton

Set in an apartment, Ana moves through reflections of a relationship that once made her feel whole, now shaped by something she cannot change. Blending humor, tenderness, and heartbreak, the play explores what it means to carry love forward.

CHARACTERS

ANA
20s-70s, near same age as Mark.

MARK
20s-70s, near same age as Ana.

NOTE: Ana and Mark are lovers. They should be about the same age. However, their age doesn't matter as much as their emotional connection. Mark can always see Ana. But Ana never sees Mark. Mark's dialogue is always delivered to Ana. But Ana should be talking to herself. They never touch.

SETTING

Modern day. Ana is in her and Mark's apartment – likely at the kitchen table.

***

Ana is sitting at the kitchen table. Mark is standing in the room. They are both already in a state of emotional angst.

ANA. I can't do this without you.

MARK. I know.

ANA. I don't want to do this without you.

(Mark looks at Ana.)

Either way we lose. Either way it will be painful – and I'll lose. I'm going to lose. I've already lost. I've never understood fighting if you know you can't win. What's the point?

MARK. Sometimes the pain of loss is lessened when the fight is well-fought.

ANA. Why do I feel like you're saying something that you want to sound wise but really just sounds like a fortune cookie?

MARK. *(laughs)* You know me well.

ANA. I like your fortune cookie comfort.

MARK. *(somberly)* I love you.

ANA. What am I going to do? Really. What am I going to do?

MARK. Ana –

ANA. Do you remember the first time we went to that Thai restaurant?

MARK. Of course. It was our second date. It was the day I knew I wanted to marry you.

ANA. I love Thai. But you had never had it.

MARK. I hadn't.

ANA. I tried to warn you.

MARK. I didn't listen.

ANA. Thai spicy is <u>not</u> the same as American spicy.

MARK. Why would I listen? Must impress girl. Eating spicy impressive.

ANA. And you ate it anyway.

MARK. Did I ever.

ANA. I thought your face was melting off.

MARK. It was.

ANA. Your eyes were watering, your nose was running.

MARK. Yeah.

ANA. I even think you might have been drooling a little.

MARK. Yup. Happens when you can't feel your face.

ANA. But you kept eating.

MARK. Sure did. Spicy impressive. Must impress girl.

ANA. It was impressive. I'm not sure I've ever told you that. I thought, in that moment, you were impressive. Stupid. But, impressive.

MARK. I knew it.

ANA. *(tearily)* Stupid. But impressive.

MARK. I'm sorry.

ANA. At the end of our meal, you asked for a fortune cookie. You didn't know Thai restaurants don't have fortune cookies.

MARK. Ana.

ANA. You were embarrassed at your mistake.

MARK. Baby.

ANA. So, you made up a fortune. "Sometimes the meal is too spicy – but good meals aren't about the food, keep eating."

MARK. I love you.

ANA. Then you said, 'I could eat you forever.'
(Ana and Mark both laugh.)

Stupid. But impressive. I knew that day I was going to marry you. I <u>knew</u> I was going to marry you.

MARK. I know.

(Mark moves toward Ana's line of sight.)

ANA. I've waited my whole life for you.

MARK. I know.

ANA. I finally found you. I opened up. <u>You</u> opened me up.

MARK. Ana.

ANA. You, you are my everything. I never thought I'd be that person. I never thought I <u>could</u> be that person. But here we are. We were happy. I was happy. I <u>was</u> happy.

MARK. I'm sorry.

ANA. God, I didn't know I was capable of that kind of connection. Not really. Not until you.

MARK. I'm so sorry.

ANA. So, what do I do now? What do I do. Theres no winning. There is no scenario where I have you. There's nothing that I can fight for. So, what do I do? What do I do?!

MARK. You eat the meal.

ANA. Shut up.

MARK. You eat the meal.

ANA. Shut up!

MARK. Baby, listen to me. You sat down with someone you love. The food burns. It hurts. Hon, I know it hurts. It's too much and it hurts. I know. But what, what were we going to do? Just, never have shared a meal? Never have been together? Never have had each other? My love, it's not about the food – it's not about what hurts. It's about the company you're in, the moments that were had, the time together.

ANA. You suck.

MARK. I know.

ANA. I can't handle this.

MARK. The burn will fade. The memory of the meal will stay.

ANA. Why do I know that you are saying something that sounds like a damn fortune cookie?! *(crying)* I wanna hear the fortune cookie.

MARK. Baby.

ANA. You know, I never needed to be impressed. I didn't. You are kind, funny, devoted – without being creepy. You are warm. You make <u>me</u> feel warm. You make me <u>feel</u>. You make me feel light. Whole.

MARK. I love you.

ANA. And now I feel like the dark will never end. Like the light was a lie, a cruel trick. What am I going to do without you?

MARK. You'll go on.

ANA. What am I going to do?!

(Long pause.)

Right now, you are there. And I am here. Alone. But I'm going to have to go back to the hospital.

MARK. I'm sorry.

ANA. I'm going to have to go back to the hospital and tell them it's okay to let you go. *(breaking into sobs)* But it's not okay. It's not. Jesus, I love you so much but fuck you.

MARK. Ana.

ANA. No. Fuck you.

MARK. Ana. You can't just live your life in a box, in a cage. You can't just let your feelings waste away from lack of use. I know it hurts, but love, love.

(Ana continues to cry.)

I know it hurts. I know. I'm so sorry. This isn't what I wanted for you – for us. But, baby, Ana, think about what we had. Think about how you let yourself be loved by me. Aren't you so glad to know you aren't as broken as you were worried you were?

ANA. I'm more broken now than I ever feared I was before.

MARK. You're not.

ANA. I hate you.

MARK. You don't. You love me. Ana. Please. I know it doesn't feel like it right now. I know, my love. But, it <u>is</u> better to have loved and lost –

ANA. I swear to god if you are in the ether about to quote Tennyson to me I will never eat Thai food again!

MARK. *(beat)* I love you.

ANA. *(still emotional but starting to reassure herself)* Okay. Okay. I'm really glad I had you.

MARK. I know.

ANA. Thank you for loving me so well.

(Ana stands up and gets herself ready to leave but then stops.)

I can't do this without you.

MARK. I know.

ANA. I don't want to do anything without you.

(Mark looks at Ana. She moves towards the door.)

ANA. Just don't really leave me.

MARK. Never.

ANA. I love you.

END OF PLAY

GATHER BY THE GHOST LIGHT is a storytelling podcast in radio theater format. Think of the Ghost Light as your campfire. Gather around and listen to stories from a variety of genres. Playwright Jonathan Cook and Devon McSherry are the hosts of the series and most of the stories you hear were originally written as stage plays and they now have been adapted to audio plays with professional voice actors and immersive sound effects. The audio dramas produced on this podcast give these talented playwrights an even wider audience for their stories. We welcome you to join us on this journey as we extend the voices of playwrights around the world!

Available wherever you get your podcasts!
For more information, please visit:
www.gatherbytheghostlight.com

Gather by the Ghost Light annual anthologies of audio plays produced on the podcast are all available through Ghost Light Publications!

Find more plays at
www.ghostlightpubs.com